Never

Ride Your Elephant to School

Henry Holt and Company, LLC
Publishers since 1866
115 West 18th Street
New York, New York 10011

Henry Holt is a registered trademark of Henry Holt and Company, LLC

Published in Canada by Fitzhenry & Whiteside Ltd.,
195 Allstate Parkway, Markham, Ontario L3R 4T8.

Library of Congress Cataloging-in-Publication Data
Johnson, Doug. Never ride your elephant to school / Doug Johnson; illustrated by Abby Carter.
Summary: A humorous account of the disadvantages of bringing an elephant into the classroom.
[1. Elephants—Fiction. 2. Schools—Fiction.]
I. Carter, Abby, ill. II. Title.
PZ7.J631715Ng 1995 [E]—dc20 94-44658

ISBN 0-8050-2880-3
First Edition—1995
Printed in the United States of America on acid-free paper. ∞

5 7 9 10 8 6

To Allen, Anne, and Gordy
— D. J.

To my mom and dad
— A. C.

Never
Ride Your Elephant
to School

Doug Johnson

Illustrated by

Abby Carter

Henry Holt and Company · New York

Never ride your elephant to school.

If you do, you will have to tie him to the bicycle rack. After he gets loose, he will ride bicycles...which is hard on the bicycles.

When he runs out of bicycles, he will get lonely and try to find you. He will trumpet quite loudly while looking for you. This could scare some of the children. Not to mention teachers.

After your elephant finds your classroom, he will sit outside and cry. When you ask the teacher if he can come in because he's lonely, the teacher will think you're joking and say, "Of course."

To revive your teacher, you will need to have the elephant squirt her with water. Elephants can squirt an awful lot of water.

By this time school will have started and it will be too late to take your elephant home. The custodian will have to find a very strong chair and desk for him. This could take until recess. The custodian won't be very happy.

Those are just some of the reasons why you should never ride your elephant to school.

But if you do, you should know...

Use caution at recess. Your elephant will want to play soccer. His tusks can cause serious problems. Never be the goalie. He can kick very, very hard.

Elephants are good at math and love to give answers. While waiting to be called on, your elephant might get excited and wiggle around in his chair. Elephants can really wiggle!

Lunchtime can be terrible. Elephants eat quite a lot. Never open a bag of peanuts, even across the room from him. An elephant's trunk can stretch a long way.

Your elephant will love the lunch break. He'll jump rope, kind of...play hopscotch...

and tetherball. Do not let him
play tetherball. He could hit the
ball too hard.

When your teacher reads a book after lunch, make sure your elephant sits in the back of the room. If he likes the story, he'll get excited and flap his ears. This can cause a strong breeze and might give the teacher problems.

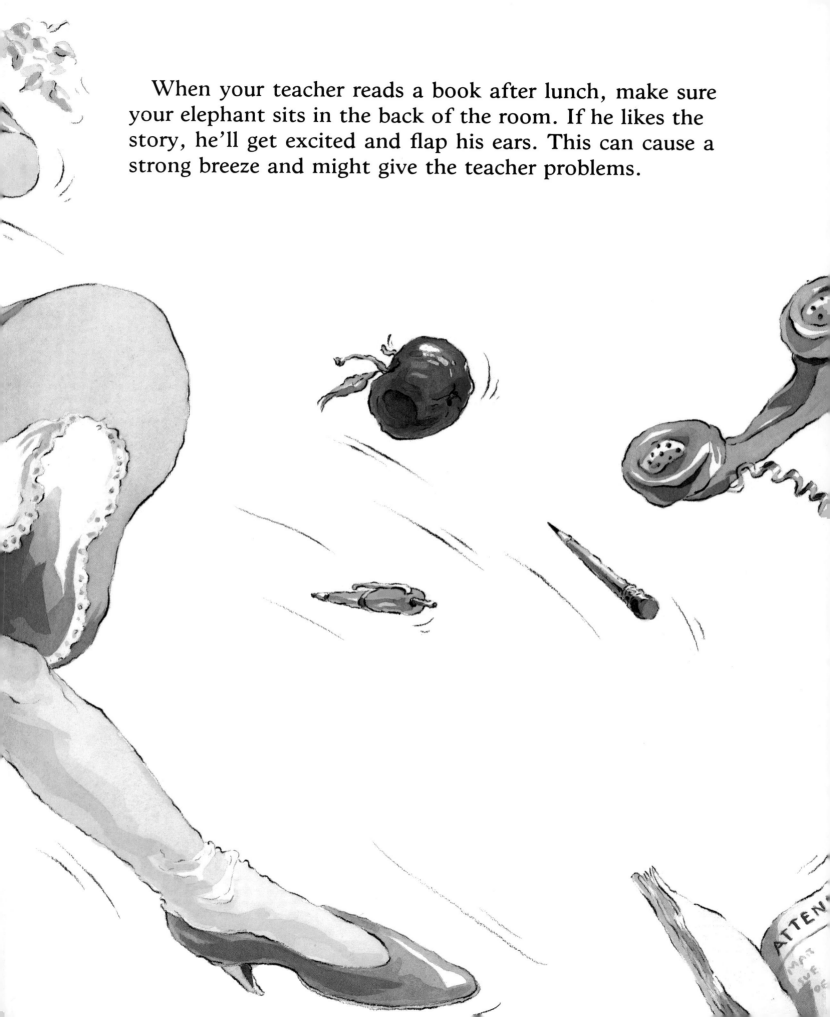

Sometimes an elephant can be useful...
...like when the school bully comes your way. Make sure your elephant is just around the corner. That way the bully won't know

. . . until it's too late!

Or during spelling. If you have a spelling bee, make sure your elephant is on your team. Your team will win. An elephant never forgets!

He'll also be very helpful with tidying up. He can blow chalk dust out of the chalk trays. Look out! You might be buried.

Overall, I'd still say never ride your elephant to school. Just think...

earthquake drills can be a problem. It'll be hard to get him under his desk.

Gym class could be hazardous. He'll want to climb the rope. Just make sure you don't stand too close. The rope might not hold up.

Your elephant will love art class and will be very creative. Be careful! Once he gets started, it might be hard for him to stop!

But if you think that's messy...wait till the end of the day. You'll have to help him clean around his desk. Elephants can be very untidy.

Warn your friends not to get in front of your elephant when school lets out. Elephants tend to rush.

Make sure you leave school right away. There will be some very upset students with wobbly bicycles.
So . . . never ever ride your elephant to school!

Ride him to the circus instead!